In memory of
Laïka
who was sent to space on 3-11-1957

THREE
SARDINES
ON A BENCH

Michaël Escoffier
Kris Di Giacomo

BERBAY
PUBLISHING

THREE SARDINES SAT ON A BENCH,
SOAKING UP THE SUMMER SUN.

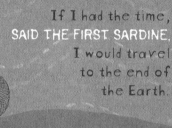

If I had the time,
SAID THE FIRST SARDINE,
I would travel
to the end of
the Earth.

I've heard that
on the other side
of the world

well-groomed horses walk on ahead.

I've heard that
at the North Pole

it is so cold that
bears eat ice-cream,
just to stay warm.

I've heard that
if you keep
looking backwards

you'll end up going back in time.

If I had the time,
SAID THE SECOND SARDINE,
I would take off and
fly amongst the clouds.

I've heard that from
up there everyone
looks like an ant.

I've heard that

on days of very high wind

you come across deer
flying as high as kites.

I've even heard that

they send dogs
into space to find
lost deer.

THE THIRD SARDINE
SAID NOTHING.

IT WAVED TO ITS

COMPANIONS

AND FLEW OFF

TO THE END OF THE EARTH.

We spend our days
sitting on this bench,
taking in the same old scene,
when there are so many
wonderful things to discover
in the world.

I've heard that there is nothing more beautiful than a pod of whales singing in the sunset.

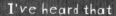
I've heard that

water rats crowd onto
the beach and stay to
enjoy the show.

I've heard that from the moon
you can watch the sun go down
several times a day.

You're right about this life of ours,

REPLIED THE SECOND SARDINE
GETTING UP FROM
THE BENCH.

I'm curious to
know what the
world looks like...

from that bench over there.

ONE SARDINE SAT ON A BENCH
SOAKING UP THE SUMMER SUN.

IT HAD A QUESTION FOR
THE SARDINE ON THE
OPPOSITE BENCH:
So what's
it like?

I've heard that

if two mirrors

reflect each other

face to face

they end up

going mad.

I've heard that

if two mirrors

reflect each other

face to face

they end up

going mad.

This edition published in 2011 by Berbay Publishing Pty Ltd
English translation © Berbay Publishing Pty Ltd 2011
www.berbaybooks.com

© L'Atelier du Poisson Soluble, 2008

Trois Sardines sur Un Banc, written by Michaël Escoffier and
illustrated by Kris Di Giacomo

English adaptation by Michael Sedunary

Edited by Bryony Oliver-Skuse

Typesetting by Kylie Hall

Printed and bound in China by Everbest Printing

National Library of Australia Cataloguing-in-Publication entry
Escoffier, Michaël

Three sardines on a bench/ Michaël Escoffier

1st ed.

ISBN 978 0 9806711 2 4 (hbk.)

For primary school age.
A821.4